"Mommy?"
"Yes, Kenny?"
"Why do I have to cut my h
Don't you like it this way?"

"Yes, I love your hair, but you don't like your hair done, Kenny."

"Mommy, do I have to go?"
"Yes Kenny. Those locs have
to go," said mommy.

"Ouch, you're hurting me!"

"That's it Kenny.
You're going to the barbershop!
Immediately!"

"Mommy, please, I don't want to go.
Can you put my hair in a ponytail?
That always works."

"Let me wash it,"
said mommy.

"Wash it? Oh no!
My eyes are going to burn.
Remember the last time
you washed my hair, I couldn't stop crying?"

"Baby, you're making it harder than it has to be. I'm not able to comb or wash your hair. I think it's a good idea to go see barber Pete."

"Mom, can I take a nap please?
All this haircut talk is making me sleepy."

"Kenny, wake up and put this on," said mommy.

"Wow! Mom, where are we going?"

1. Find Pete's barber shop.
2. Find the colorful cape with his name.
3. Find the spaceship chair.
4. A special treat.

"We are going on a scavenger hunt!"

"It sounds like fun! Call me detective Kenny!"

"Up the block and down the street! We're off to find barber Pete!"

"Look mom, I found the barber shop.
See it reads "Pete's Barbershop"."

"Good job, Kenny!
Here is a star.
Put it in the box next
to the number one."

"What's next on the list?" mommy asked Kenny. "The spaceship seat is next," said Kenny.

"I spy with my bright eyes a spaceship seat. Sticker, please!"

"Good job, Kenny, two down two to go," said mommy.

"Can you help me find the cape mommy?"
  asked Kenny. "This one is too hard for me."
"Sure, baby. How about we ask Mr. Pete?"
"Mr. Pete, can you help us find the cape, please?"
  said Kenny

"A spaceship cape just for Kenny!"
said Mr. Pete

"Look mommy it says "Kenny"!"
"I see, baby. Now sit still for Mr. Pete,"
said mommy.

"All done!" said Mr. Pete
"Wow, mommy, look at me!"

"Thank you, Mr. Pete!"
"Thank you, Kenny!"

"Good job, detective Kenny!
Here is your treat!"
"Thanks, mom! This is neat.
Can we do this again next week?"

"Be a good boy and we'll see.
Say "bye" to Mr. Pete."
"Goodbye, Mr. Pete! See you
next week!"

THE END